MODERN RELATIONSHIPS

PRIYA GOPAL

I dedicate this book to Garima, my darling daughter.

Contents

Foreword

My observations now, have made me think twice before jumping into any comment about any person within the family, friends, peer group or social media. Today's man-woman relationship can be very varied, more meaningful, more respectful, non-commercial, more equal and with more mutual respect towards each other. The adjusting, all rounder, financially independent, well-mannered and understanding spouse is the one who everybody wants. And today in the wide wild world, you get them too. Reading this book will make you more aware about what to expect and be prepared for the mindsets in big cities around the globe.

Preface

This book has got basically two stories. The foundations of both the stories are today's modern city life. It challenges age-old myths, and are more attractive, real and can be emulated.

Modern Relationships_1: It has got seven parts. The story revolves around Sonali and Adarsh. The story is not filmy at all. Sonali wanted to do her PhD in Microbiology. She wanted to be a career-woman. A beautiful no-nonsense girl that she was, she rejected three marriage proposals from well-to-do guys because they wanted their wives to be home-makers. Finally, she met Adarsh, a SSC pass taxi-driver. He was a man of integrity and kept her grounded. Their marital life ofcourse had shocking range of hassels. But true love, triumphs all.

Modern Relationships_2: Prostitutes destroy a man's life. They corrupt your brain and eat up your wealth slowly but surely. You lose respect in society and the woman turns you into a joker and a good-for-nothing simpleton. Well, grannies and mummies speak a lot, but even in today's modern India and for the mutually respecting men and women, there can be a story which touches your heart. Business tycoon Arvind Kaushal and after his death, his only son Devesh both fall head over heals in love and are totally smitten by the prostitute Antara. Her family moved away from her. Her daughters Sonali and Namrata trust their aunt Aarti more, because she was a respectable lady. The story has six parts and who is right ? who is wrong ? Whom should we support ? will be the three major questions in your heart once you read the story.

Acknowledgements

I thank my husband for putting up with my erratic work schedules. I thank my daughter Garima for being my honest critic and my father for supporting me in every way possible.

MODERN RELATIONSHIPS_1

CHAPTER TWO

PART 1

"You look gorgeous in this ghagra-choli. This makeup, this hairstyle, wah ! Subhaan Allah. I know why you're so happy today. I know haan, don't try to hide anything from me." teased Vidisha to her friend Sonali. A blushing Sonali said in reply "Today is the last day of Navratri. After this we may not meet. I plan to let Adarsh know the feelings of my heart today itself." A shocked Vidisha reiterated "But you just met eight days ago. Do you know him that well that you plan to marry him ? See, let me tell you, he just studied uptill tenth grade/standard and is a taxi driver by profession. A lone child of his parents, he belongs to lower middle class." Sonali, with a firm look on her face, turned towards her and said about her final decision "So what, I still want to marry him".

On the dance-ground, Sonali took Adarsh to a side and let him know of her feelings for him. He was not prepared for this talk and answered with a shocked expression "But you know you're MSc- microbiology Mumbai University topper and I'm a college dropout. How will it match ?." "Love and respect for each other and each other's careers should always be there. It is not about belittling, it's only about working hard. See... see... see the earlier three arranged marriage proposals, I've rejected because they wanted me just to be a housewife. You understand why ?" explained Sonali. He just turned and ran away from there as fast as he could, straight to his house.

Contrary to what she had expected, she was still sleeping on her bed, when she suddenly got up on hearing many people talking outside. As she stealthily tried to check what was happening outside, she saw Adarsh feeding boondi laddoos to her father. Her heart started beating faster. Then after four months, both of them were married as per maharashtrian rituals.

As per what she wanted, she started pursuing her PhD in microbiology.

On her first year out of her two year course, she felt fishy regarding a fellow research-scientist working next to her. Her guide was Dr Manik Verma. The scientist on which she had doubt was fifty eight year old Dr Devdhar Muzumdar. He was doing meticulous and massive research on certain fully extinct very dangerous and harmful microorganisms, which actually he wasn't supposed to do.

Four weeks passed, then on one day, she overheard Dr Devdhar talking to his younger daughter on his phone "You don't worry Neha. We'll finish off the Talwalkars. I'll not allow even a single member of their family to live..."

Sonali got scared. At home after dinner, she tried to tell her husband "Adarsh, I'm... I'm very sure that some mishap will surely happen if we don't report the matter to the police." Adarsh, not taking it seriously said "Tomorrow you have to get up early in the morning. So go to sleep". But she couldn't get a wink of sleep. At half past twelve midnight, she woke up her husband saying "We have to go to the police. There is no other way out". So both of them went to the local police station. Dr Devdhar was arrested and in the police torture room, he became a ball of anger and hatred. He used cuss words against the Talwalkar family "My... my elder daughter Soumya, who was the apple of my eye, killed herself because Mayuresh Talwalkar refused to marry her after nine years of relationship. His mother used such harsh words on my... on my daughter that, she was totally destroyed inside. So I'm reviving the deadliest virus in the history of the world and will finish off the Talwalkar family. I'm in the final stages of my research and their death knell will happen soon. I'm not scared of you guys. My daughters are important. Nothing... nothing else matters to me. You heard it right, nothing else matters to me". The police let him off with a stern warning. But unlike what he thought, they were keeping a strict vigil on him and handled the case very carefully. After three days, the police shot him dead in the research laboratory itself, because he refused to budge and there was no other way out for them also.

One week after seeing her dad's deadbody, Neha's mental health was impaired. So she was admitted to the nearby mental hospital.

Sonali was given a medal for her bravery in Red fort, Delhi in a very prestigious and well-televised event. Adarsh and her in-laws also had accompanied her over there and they, especially Adarsh felt extremely proud of her.

CHAPTER THREE

PART 2

There was a girl Manisha Pratap who used to come driving her own car. The perfect dress and to compliment it perfect make-up and hairstyle. Soon everyone knew who was she. She was the reigning chief minister Dhananjay Pratap's daughter from his first wife Nirmala. When she was one year old, her father divorced her mother and later on married again. Sonali thought, it was not good to come close to her, what if you rub her the wrong way ? But Sonali was a topper. So how could anyone ignore her ? She herself gave the invitation card of her birthday party to her. Sonali and Adarsh went to the party, thoroughly enjoyed and both came back before late.

Then just two months before the PhD degree was officially over, there was a breaking news which shell-shocked everyone. The chief minister's wife, his three children from her were killed in a car-crash in the US. It was a big jolt to the chief minister Mr Pratap the man himself. After all the due procedures were over, he called up his daughter Manisha to stay in his bungalow henceforth and also begin her political career as his successor. She agreed. Sonali's in-laws and even neighbours started chit-chating behind her back and even openly advised her to cash-in on her political connections. Sonali finished her PhD course and got the job of an associate professor. She started earning well.

Then one day, Manisha called up to congratulate Sonali on finishing her doctorate. Manisha asked Sonali whether she can be of any help to her. On the advise of her mother-in-law, Sonali told Manisha that her mother-in-law has always remained tense because her son doesn't have a good job. So Manisha offered him a job of a party worker. Adarsh obliged.

Six months later, during lunch-break at the university, Sonali was going through her mobile and was shocked to find a WhatsApp message from her husband. It was sent twenty minutes ago, when she was taking class. She was shocked to read what was written on it.

"Manisha madam has changed after she became the chief minister. Her father was good, but not in any way the daughter. The success and the power has gone into her head. She is a thorough narcissist now. You won't believe what happened today. She today called me to her cabin alone and asked me to become her keep. I refused the offer. So she chucked me out of the job and threatened me that she'll throw me and my family out of Maharashtra. She also insulted me saying I'm uneducated and so keep my head down and accept and follow whatever the chief minister is asking me to do. I again refused. She flared up and said that she'll cut off the heads of all my family members. So the first thing I've done is go out of Maharashtra. Soon my train will reach its destination."

A shocked Sonali immediately called him up. He just uttered two words:

"Vitthal mama's house"

and cut the call. She called him up twice after that, but the line didn't connect. Then as she immediately rushed back home, after ten minutes, her father-in-law called her up.

She told him only the following few words-
"Please sasuma and you immediately head to Vitthal mama's house"
Then she switched off her mobile. All four met in Kerala. Vitthal mama and his wife stayed there. They were also shocked by what happened in Mumbai.
There was a politician Ramam Nair who was a strong man in Kerala. Sonali and Adarsh met him after taking his appointment. But he flatly refused to help. Then Sonali and her husband, disappointed went back to Vitthal mama's house.
At half past eleven midnight, the door bell rang. Vitthal mama opened the door. It was Manisha with her fifteen men dressed in white clothes. Sonali and Adarsh also woke up because of her shrill and very strong and confident voice. "I'll sleep with your husband, what'll you do ? You have no idea who I am. You have no idea of my power and reach. Tell your husband to accept the job of sleeping with me." shouted Manisha at Sonali. Then Manisha turned to the direction of Adarsh, who was standing next to his wife. "You are my keep. I'll pay you well. I'LL PAY YOU WELL, I'LL PAY YOU WELL" shouting at the top of her shrill voice, she started ripping apart his button-downed shirt with full force. Then the top button of the shirt fell down along with the bloodied head of the deadbody of Manisha. She was shot on the head by former chief minister of Maharashtra Dhananjay Pratap who was also her father. Kerala strong man Ramam Nair stood besides him. "I'm totally shocked by her behaviour. I'm sorry for the problems faced by you and your family". As tears trickled down his eyes, from his mobile he made a call to the police and surrendered himself. In court it was proved that nobody other than Mr Dhananjay could control her. She was power-mad and

misused her position to do heinous and horrible things. So since there was no other way out, Mr Dhananjay had to shoot her". The sad father was left free. He adopted a girl-child from an orphanage in Mumbai and retired from politics.

Sonali, Adarsh and her in-laws, heaved a sigh of relief and returned back to Mumbai.

CHAPTER FOUR

PART 3

Two years passed. Sonali was two months pregnant. She was transferred to the biggest research centre in India, TIRO research center in Bengaluru. She went there. All arrangements were made by the company so that she was safe and healthy. Adarsh's mom wanted him also to stay over there. She didn't believe in long distance relationships. And since they were expecting a baby, she didn't want Sonali to be alone. Adarsh took Sonali's mother Kantabai to Bengaluru and then he was relieved.

On the contrary to what she had thought while getting Sonali married to Adarsh, Kantabai was fully sure now that SSC pass son-in-law was a wrong decision. Sonali's father Shambhunath also started staying in his hugely successful daughter's house and kept pestering Sonali and her mother to get a divorce, and marry a more successful and educated man. But like before, Sonali was very sure about Adarsh that he was the perfect man for her.

Then it was the time for her delivery. Adarsh was there in the hospital with his mother Shobha too. All through the hours in the hospital ie before the birth of child and till the mother and baby were discharged, Kantabai and Shambhunath kept insulting Shobha repeatedly. Once when the later broke into tears, Adarsh came there and asked the reason behind it. Then Shambhunath insulted Adarsh very badly calling him uneducated and unfit for his daughter. With moist eyes, Adarsh took his mother and shifted to a nearby lodge. Adarsh used to come to Bengaluru every three months and stay in the quarters of his wife and baby girl Ranjita for a week and then returned back to Mumbai after that. He was not on talking terms with his in-laws. Sonali was too busy with her job as a scientist in the research lab and had to give her time and energy to her toddler too. She did sense a cold-war between her husband and her parents, but nor had the time or the energy to intervene.

Three years passed. It was baby Ranjita's third birthday. First Sonali woke up at six a.m. She was surprised to see the whole house decorated with flowers, banners, balloons and satin ribbons. All over the house, in each wall, there were big sized invitation cards pasted. It was the invitation for Ranjita's birthday party in the main Bengaluru hotel at seven in the evening.

Then in the hotel after visiting it personally, Shambhunath, Kantabai and Sonali came to know what it was and what Adarsh had planned. The name of the hotel was 'Hotel Ranjita'. It was a nice simple and spacious place. "Sonali and my baby girl Ranjita, this place is for you. I've worked my ass off to buy this place, furnish and do its interiors. For three grueling years I learnt to cook all south-Indian foods. My mom used to wake up the entire night to taste and give her inputs to the food prepared by me. It's her and mine joint efforts. I'm the cook here. I've three servants. My father has come forward to take care of the cash counter. If on any day I'm not there, then my mom is also fully trained to cook delicious south-Indian food. So today is the first day of it being open to the public. I'm happy and I hope

Ranjita when she grows up likes it too. Sonu(Sonali) do you like this place ?" With a bright smile she hugged her husband and took the mic in her hands and said "I love this place and adore this place. Today, on this beautiful occasion I've turned from a proud mother to an even more prouder wife. I love you Adarsh".

Sonali feeding medu wada through a fork to Adarsh pic was framed and hung on the living room wall of her quarters. Shambhunath and Kantabai went back to Mumbai. Sonali's in-laws moved in. That night when everyone were peacefully sleeping, in the middle of the night, Sonali wrote in her blog-

"I've achieved everything, touch wood".

CHAPTER FIVE

PART 4

One year passed with full marital bliss. Then came the challenges.

There was a call on the intercom, asking all residents to be present at 7PM. Sonali and Adarsh attended the meeting. There, there were three policemen present. They circulated the photo of a fifteen year old girl, Meeta Shanbhaug, who stayed in the tower next to the quarters and was missing since the past four days. Suddenly, Adarsh said to the police that four days ago, the same girl sat right outside his hotel, fully drenched in rain and with tears in her eyes. His servant Ashish first spotted her there. He alerted Adarsh. Even though she didn't answer any of his questions, she drank the tea which he offered. Half an hour later, when he came back to check on her, there was the empty cup and saucer kept over there, she was gone.

Three days later the girl was found and brought by the police to the police station. Her parents and elder brother were doctors. She complained to the police that her family were putting huge pressure on her and treated her very badly. They wanted her also to become a doctor. But she hated academics. She had passed SSC exam and scored only 50%. So she herself went to the red-light area in the forbidden locality. She with plain expression on her face, claimed to have slept with three men. The police reprimanded her parents for putting too much pressure on their daughter. Tears rolled down her mother's eyes. Her father assured the police that hence forth they won't put undue pressure on their daughter. They accepted her back. But as her father said to the police, she was separately kept in the flat two blocks away. The flat was in the joint-names of her father and mother. She was arranged to stay there with a full-time servant Laxmi. The police agreed. The news spread. Sonali and Adarsh felt sorry for the girl. On the advise of Sonali, Adarsh offered the girl, the job of a waitress in his hotel. She agreed.

People around did know that she came from a family of doctors. But Adarsh's offer would bring positivity to her life, that's what her mother felt. So the work began.

After eleven months, she personally went and gifted a small Lord Ganesha idol to Ranjita on her birthday. Her salary was far less than the money spent on her by her family. But as Dr Pratibha, her mother felt, one or two years of free and non-toxic life, would change her attitude towards life and she'll herself agree to do something productive. Her mother kept tab on her regularly, by talking to both Laxmi and Adarsh at regular intervals.

CHAPTER SIX

PART 5

Three months later, like every day, at 7AM Adarsh himself opened the shutters of his hotel. But was shocked to see in the pathway to the hotel's kitchen, lied the body of Meeta. She was lying in a pool of blood. He could very visibly see that her throat was slit and she laid still on the floor. He panicked and called the police. He was the person along with his wife, who fought with the world and agreed to give her shelter. Then he called up his wife and asked her to come to the hotel immediately. On the phone he couldn't explain her, she was also perplexed, but got ready to go there. The police reached the hotel before her. They cordoned off the area. The body was taken to the hospital for postmortem and the forensic team started their work. Adarsh and his wife, were both taken for questioning. Adarsh had left the hotel at 10PM the previous day and went directly to the quarters. The quarters' watchman confirmed this. He was seen in the CCTV footage also. Even Sonali was also seen in the 6:30 PM footage. So both of them were left free.

Adarsh told to the police, during the interrogation, what Meeta had told during her selection, that she had done prostitution with three men. So the nearby red-light area was also combed. Revealing the names of their customers was against the brothel norm. But when Sayyed Ali, her pimp was tortured in the police torture room, he revealed the name of the three customers.

The CCTV recordings were taken for examination by the police on the first day itself. After seven days, Adarsh went personally to the police station, asking for permission to reopen the hotel. The police told that from the next day onwards, the hotel can be opened for the customers.

The next morning, only Ashish ie one servant came to the job. Ashish revealed to his boss Adarsh that the other servant Ram was zeroed by the police for the murder of Meeta. Ram was a very normal guy who couldn't kill anyone, Adarsh was sure. He along with his wife and lawyer Iyengar went to the police station. After speaking for a while with Adarsh, the concerned boss, the police inspector Laxman Gowda, called his lawyer and wife to the next room. He told them in a hush-hush tone "Actually a very big politician's son was her regular customer and got the murder done, in a fit of rage since she refused to serve her body to him. She had also given horrible cuss-words to the man himself. He is a big man. So Ram agreed to go to jail, in return for a hefty sum. Ram's two kids will be sent to an expensive private school and the fees and their total expenditure will be borne by the politician himself. Ram and his family agreed. Ram's family was also given a spacious flat in his name in the Whitefield area. So now Ram is in jail instead of the big man. This happens ma'am. This is what life is all about." Then the lawyer was asked to back off by Sonali. She went to the outer room, caught Adarsh by his elbow and pulled him out of the police station. "The matter is solved. YOU DON'T INTERFERE. Hire another person in both Ram and Meeta's place. Okay ?". Reading her face, he also agreed to cooperate with his wife and said "okay".

CHAPTER SEVEN

PART 6

Three years passed. In the first year the hotel business ran well. But in the preceding two years, there were losses. Adarsh's in-laws were keeping track of how his business performed. Once, when they were having dinner, his father-in-law pointed out before everybody that he was earning lesser than he used to earn as a taxi driver. Adarsh smiled and only said "I'll think of a way out of this". Sonali smiled but she didn't say anything.

After two weeks, she during lunch break at the lab, called him over to Diwan's college of engineering which was a newly constructed one. Both of them together went there and spoke to the authorities. It was a state of the art college with all the modern amenities. Within some days, Adarsh's chaat counter was approved by the authorities. So it just took off. The students just loved the superb experience of puri with the masala melting in their mouth. After ten months, Adarsh shut his hotel and focused fully on his chaat counter. On Ranjita's birthday at home, he himself served, along with the kiddo friends of Ranjita, his in-laws too. As soon as his mother-in-law finished all six puris of ragda puri, she had tears of joy in her eyes. She said "I love my son-in-law more than anything in this world. No matter what challenge God puts before him, he just puts his life into everything he does. I'm proud of Adarsh. I want another plate, beta". The father-in-law had a sunken expression. Sonali just smiled.

Adarsh started earning very well. The earnings crossed way beyond than it was expected.

CHAPTER EIGHT

PART 7

Sonali had a brilliant family at home. So like always, she informed her husband that she was working on something very new and important. After three months, she one day came home early and on phone itself conveyed that she was taking her family out for a mughlai dinner.

The family attended the dinner and had a sumptuous meal. But all through the dinner she was only eating and smiling. She didn't say anything else.

At home before dozing off she told Adarsh that after one month, she was going to the US and the trip was work-related.

She went to the US. Eight months later, at night 2AM, Adarsh's mobile rang. "I've been selected for the prestigious Mobel prize for my work in microbiology and the discovery of Wertopus organism, a microorganism which eats up only Cancer viruses. It preys upon Cancer virus. The team of Mobel prize went through my discovery and research and just five minutes before, I got the information from the Mobel authorities. I just feel great." She expressed her joy on the phone.

Eighteen days later, while she was receiving the medal, she thanked the chairman of the prize authorities first and then came the acceptance speech:

"I love my husband. He is a gem"
As she descended down from the stage, she hugged her husband with moist eyes. He too got emotional and with tears of joy flowing down his cheeks, hugged her back.

MODERN RELATIONSHIPS_2

PART 1

"Have you gone mad ? What about ME ? What about Sonali and Namrata ? Do you know the impact of this ? This will totally destroy our family. You leave that rich man. YOU LEAVE THAT RICH MAN." shouted Neeraj Kalsekar on his wife Antara. "What if I don't ? I'm leaving you. That's what I've decided. He can give me all the luxuries which you can't even imagine." said Antara in a firm strong voice. Mr Kalsekar immediately left the house. Tears flowed down his eyes. But he didn't utter any more word. He filed for divorce the next day itself. The girls, Sonali 16 and Namrata 14 were put in the boarding school in Kodaikanal, Tamil Nadu. Four months later the warden Mrs Aurora of their luxurious school, called both the girls to her office, where she was sitting in her night dress. It was well past midnight. As soon as both the girls came there, she spoke, "Your mother had called me on my mobile. Your father Mr Kalsekar has been admitted to the hospital. He is serious. He wants to see both of you as early as possible.". Their mother Antara had sent a sportscar with a driver to bring the girls to Mumbai.

Both the girls saw that their father was ailing. He had suffered a heart-attack. He asked his elder daughter Sonali to take a chair and sit besides his bed. Tears were flowing down the younger daughter Namrata's cheeks. Sonali was very tense. She followed her father's instructions and sat besides him. He said "Sonali, you're the elder one. So you can understand my plight. Listen carefully. Your mother doesn't love us. For money and luxurious life, she has crushed our family life beneath her feet. That rich man Arvind Kaushal is important for her, not us. She cannot be trusted at all. So your Aarti aunty and her husband Manoj should be your go to people. In case of any issue or any decision making, only these two should be consulted, not your mother. Aarti is my younger sister. I've seen her grow up. She and her husband, both have got a clear heart. Both are educated and well to do. They will guide you in the best way." Sonali promised her dad that she'll do likewise and guide and take care of her younger sister. Suddenly he started panting very heavily. Sonali pressed the emergency button. One nurse and doctor rushed to the room. Both the sisters were told to remain outside the room. Namrata stood, whereas Sonali sat on the bench, both having tears in their eyes. Aarti was called inside. After fifteen minutes, the doctor came out and conveyed to the girls that their dad was no more. After the cremation, both the girls went back to their boarding school. Both the girls never spoke directly to their mother. The sisters were close. After her BBM(Bachelor of Business Management), taking the advice of their aunt Aarti and Manoj uncle, she secured admission in Harvard University for her MBA. Her mother was just sent the bills, which Antara paid from the huge amount that the business tycoon Arvind Kaushal was paying her.

As a part-time job in the US, she babysat a rich man Lawrence Johnson's daughter Lili. Two years later, she received the result of her MBA degree. She had passed with flying colours. An excited Sonali first informed her sister in India on the phone. Then she called up Aarti and informed her also. She went to the nearby food store and purchased nice home-made chocolates and first gave it to her boss. He first became happy and then was shocked that now she'll take up a corporate job and quit her babysitting job. He became mad with the tension that who will take care of his daughter ? He TRUSTED no one as far as his daughter, the apple of his eye was concerned. Suddenly he turned towards Sonali and said "Listen carefully. Two months ago my younger brother George had a very bitter breakup with his girlfriend. And... and I know you are a very nice girl. I have seen you since the past two years very closely. It would be great if you marry my brother. Please date him. If both of you like each other, then... then you may marry. I'll make you an independent entrepreneur. I've got the money. This is a VERY GOOD OFFER. Take it up. Life will be great." Four months later, Sonali took the child with her to work. It had a nanny. But the child was before her eyes only. Sonali got together eleven Indian women and men and started a farsan and Indian sweets' business. The food items were prepared by these workers and then packed and distributed to all the departmental stores. Eight months into it, the Americans just loved it. The business was registered in her name, which made her beam with pride, although the name of the business was 'Lili Indian foods'.

CHAPTER ELEVEN

PART 2

Three years passed. Now, the Johnson family was so happy with Sonali that, a month ago, George proposed to her with a diamond ring. She accepted. It was a practice since day one that daily before going to sleep, she had adhered to a practice that she used to have a practise of speaking to her aunt Aarti, who stayed in Delhi for five minutes and a video call to her younger sister Namrata, who was a Science professor in Mumbai.

Both the sisters earned well. But the major and heinous issues faced by her family early in her mind, scarred her for ever. She informed about her impending marriage only to her sister Namrata, Aarti aunty and Manoj uncle. She didn't speak to her mother at all. Monetarily her estranged mother was supporting her since the year before. But about her boyfriend and impending marriage, she didn't inform her mother, who she took as a maneater without any moral values. Arvind Kaushal has been dead for two years now. But whatever his father left off, the spoilt brat son Devesh Kaushal took over. Now Antara was sleeping with her master's son and similarly getting paid for it just like before. There was a big full wall poster of Antara with her two daughters photo taken on Sonali's sixth birthday party. It had so much laughter and happiness written all over it. The estranged mother very well knew that her daughters hated her and regarded her as a characterless woman. She had no guts to herself call on her daughters' mobile. But like her late husband she was also sure about Aarti's parenting abilities. She considered Aarti as a very intelligent woman. Antara had properties worth crores. She also had very expensive diamond jewellery collection. All these jewellery were gifted by her boss Devesh. His mother Aruna devi hated Antara. Aruna devi blamed Antara for causing a rift in her marriage to Arvind Kaushal and also blamed Antara for her only son Devesh's no marriage plans. Infact, on one sunday, in their mansion her son came home at seven in the morning after spending a full night having fun with Antara and sitting just opposite to his mother, said "I want to marry Antara. I had this feeling deep in my heart when I happened to see her nude serving whisky to dad in the other house. I love her. The feeling is very deep and I'll marry her only and no one else. I've decided this and since you are my mother, informed you beforehand." Aruna devi got mad with anger. She still patiently waited for her son to go to his bedroom. As soon as he left, she took her mobile and called up a sharpshooter Haney Khan and gave the supari of Antara to him. Then she with a smile went to her room and had a deep satisfied slumber.

After a full eight hour sleep, she got up, took a bath and took her car and drove to a big sweet mart. She ate six varieties of sweets that day and came back home. When she checked her mobile, which she had left at home, she saw six missed calls from her son. She called him back. He was wailing loudly on the phone call. He informed her that when he visited Antara for his daily dose of s** as usual, he saw her hanging on a noose tied to the ceiling fan. He was the first one to see the deadbody. Aruna devi conveyed her condolences and tried to pacify her son. He came home after full forty-eight hours. He cried the whole day there also resting his head on his mother's lap. After two weeks the police also closed the case. The late Antara's daughters and other members of the family also didn't attend her funeral. They didn't want to get linked in public with a prostitute. The funeral was taken care of by Devesh only.

CHAPTER TWELVE

PART 3

Devesh changed after Antara's death. He planned to sell off their family business and join the hippie-sadhu culture in Mathura, Uttar Pradesh. His mom came to know of it. She took over the family business. Like always, without listening to Aruna devi, he left for Mathura for good. It was difficult for Aruna devi, who was primarily a housewife for twenty-eight years to take on business head on. Her best friend Ms Laajwanti Dixit was the principal of a reputed Management college just a few blocks away from her house. She called her up and told her that she wanted a very intelligent and hardworking student to look into the business and the person should be the one with integrity whom she could trust to a great extent. Ms Dixit asked her to give her time of two weeks to which Aruna devi agreed. Finally Juhi Mitra was the post-grad who was selected. She took over the business head on. "I loved Juhi's attitude towards life. The grit inside her was commendable. So I selected her." told Ms Dixit to Aruna devi. The business picked up speed. The turnover increased along with respect in the industry.

Three years passed. In a well publicized interview to Zobes India business magazine, she told her long term goals was to join politics and lead India even. The company was going great guns. Three more years passed. One day at six in the evening she and her parents came to visit Aruna devi. The later didn't expect them to come. Juhi's mother told to Aruna devi "Our girl has grown up. We have come here to give you the invitation of Juhi's marriage. She is now a famous name in the field of business. We feel proud of our daughter. The bridegroom is politician Shiv Rajan's son Aniket. Please come to the wedding, you along with your family". With a smile, Aruna devi agreed. As soon as they left, Aruna devi put her face on the sofa cushion and cried. This was because basically she didn't have a family. Her husband had died and her only son was a hippie-sadhu in Mathura. She decided to go solo to the wedding. She began thinking and her mind was surrounded by horrible and worthless thoughts. Finally at night one am, she called up her son. The manager of a hotel Mohan Sharma picked up the phone. He told her that just two months ago hippie-sadhu Devesh had left the place and gone to Kashi. The manager took the wedding invitation message and disconnected the call.

Two months later, Aruna devi went solo to the wedding. When she looked back as to who was standing behind her in the line to congratulate the couple, she just was taken aback. It was her very own son. Devesh had a full grown beard and it was quite clear from the way he looked that he had not taken bath since the past one year. He came there dressed shabbily in saffron robes with a big trishul with dumroo in one hand and a copper vessel filled with water on the other hand. He had a very messy waist-length hair, which had become thick and even they looked unwashed and uncombed since the past one year. All eyes were on him, the guests felt scared. Soon without thinking or enquiring much, he was forcibly dragged and thrown out of the main gate by three of the venue's watchmen together. Aruna devi was silent and tears flowed down her cheeks.

CHAPTER THIRTEEN

PART 4

From the gate of the wedding venue itself, she called up their family doctor Dr H Burman, and asked what she should do in such a situation ? He said that he'll visit Aruna devi in her bungalow at seven in the evening.

He kept his words. He was accompanied by his brother Dr Brijesh Burman who was a psychiatrist. After discussing everything for one full hour, it was decided that a very effective and strong counselling may do what his mother couldn't do in so many years. Aruna devi was of the firm opinion that she doesn't want her son to go back to Mathura again. He has to HAS TO mend his ways. Devesh was forcibly dragged to the hospital. He was tied to an iron chair very firmly, cleaned with water and lots of disinfectant and soap. His full hair, beard and moustache was also fully shaved off. The Burman brothers got him admitted and the rigourous counselling session began. After three weeks, he was freed. Dr Brijesh Burman after the full successful treatment was done, called up Aruna devi and spoke "Your son Devesh is now hale and hearty, both physically and mentally. He wants to become a film-director after reaching home. That is what he has said to us over here." Aruna devi had moist eyes.

The next morning she personally went to the hospital and

brought him back. He looked healthy and also spoke like a well-educated Mumbai-bred man.

Two months later, he got admission in a reputed film-school.

Five years passed, the apple of his mother's eye, Devesh had secured the degree and had directed two films. The films were released and appreciated by the media.

PART 5

Namrata was an avid movie-lover. When news regarding Devesh Kaushal's first directorial came out, she told her husband regarding the same. Both of them and their five year old daughter Seema went to the multiplex and saw the movie. Namrata liked the movie. She saw Devesh's interview too. He spoke at length about how he had written the script and how he shot the film and that the Starfare best director award meant the world to him. He also smiled at the host and told that service to audience was service to God. This was interesting for Namrata. She informed her elder sister Sonali about the new surprising news. Sonali who was older during the time their father died, still blamed Arvind and Devesh Kaushal for ruining their family life. She did say in a very effective and firm tone that Devesh was always a spoilt brat who didn't know what to do with the enormous amount of wealth his family had. She told Namrata very clearly that people with such kind of vices never change and both he and his late father were madly addicted to prostitutes. Sonali's daughter Shobita had come to Mumbai for her summer holidays. Acting was her passion and without informing her own parents on the guidance of Namrata, she participated in an acting competition. She came first in it. It was organized by starfare magazine 2022. She was selected by the casting agent Minku to act in Devesh's most anticipated third movie. When Namrata got this latest information, she got scared, scared of Sonali. Namrata couldn't say 'yes', she couldn't say 'no'. But staying true to God, she informed her husband Nikhil regarding this and herself took the bundle of talent Shobita to the producer's office. Shobita's role in the film was very important and meaty. She was the supporting actress. As soon as her shoot was fully over, Namrata sent her back to the US, back to her parents and it was school time too.

The post-production, marketing and promotion was fully done AND THE FILM WAS RELEASED. Shobita was very much praised in the movie. Along with that the director Devesh was also praised for his hardwork and perfection in the craft.

CHAPTER FIFTEEN

PART 6

The news reached Sonali. She came to India all by herself and with full rage stormed the set of an other movie where Devesh's friend Sunil was shooting, and slapped Devesh in full public view. It immediately became the fodder for the media. Stories right since Sonali and Namrata's childhood started doing the rounds of the media. Devesh's mad and rash dedication and endless lust for their late mother Antara who was a prostitute ie his mistress was splashed across the media. The issue was so spicy and red hot that Devesh was mocked upon by the name 'vagina ka deewana(crazy of vagina)' by the media.

In the Starfare awards the next year, the movie was nominated in all the top categories. But because of endless hounding by the media, Devesh didn't come out of his house. He won, his film also won many awards, but the widespread furore, insult and mockery dampened the ace-director's mind.

As soon as the Starfare award function was over, Aruna devi got the news that the film was widely appreciated by the general audience and the critics, but her son was sad because of the way the paparazzi sensationalized his old personal life, she immediately drove to her son's house. She cajoled and rebuilt the wounded spirit of her son.

Two months later the national film awards were held in the prestigious Rashtrapati Bhawan in Delhi. There Aruna devi and her son Devesh sat besides each other. Right next to them Shobita and Namrata were seated. The individual awards were being announced. Devesh came on stage along with his mother and with moist eyes said "This award belongs to my mother shrimati Aruna devi. There is no match to her dedication, towards taking me here from the gutter that I was lying in. And yes, my beloved Antara, my life is for you. I know you are seeing this from above, no other woman will be part of my life and you'll be forever and ever the only one. Thank you". In the 'best supporting actress' award category, there was a very humungous round of applause when Shobita's name was announced. Shobita came to the stage with her aunty dearest Namrata and said "Thank you very much my fans. Namrata aunty you're God to me. Please please all you grownups end up the feud and hatred in the family. Please see art in this, not a means to criticize somebody who was deeply in love. Let bygones be bygones, please. The old times, bad or good will never come back. I'm not forcing anyone to hug and be bumchums, but within each of our dignity, let's patch up and celebrate this amazing festival of talent, FILMS. And last but not the least mom, Namrata aunty is not bad. It was an intelligent decision and coming back to this award, I'll treasure it for my life time. Thank you".